Where is Pim?

Lena and Olof Landström

Where is Pim?

GECKO PRESS

Pim wants to fly.

Pim is flying high.

It took Pim!

Where is Pim?

Pom is looking.
The dog is looking too.

Is that Pim?

No, that's a bag.

Is that Pim?

No, that's a can.

Pi-im! calls Pom.
Woof! calls the dog.

Pim is gone.

Oh no! The pond…

Poor Pim.

A sock!

But where is Pim?

Pim!

Pim doesn't want to fly any more today.
Pom doesn't either.

This edition first published in 2015 by Gecko Press
PO Box 9335, Marion Square, Wellington 6141, New Zealand
info@geckopress.com

First American edition published in 2015 by Gecko Press USA, an imprint of Gecko Press Ltd.
A catalog record for this book is available from the US Library of Congress.

Distributed in the United States and Canada by Lerner Publishing Group, www.lernerbooks.com
Distributed in the United Kingdom by Bounce Sales and Marketing, www.bouncemarketing.co.uk
Distributed in Australia by Scholastic Australia, www.scholastic.com.au
Distributed in New Zealand by Random House NZ, www.randomhouse.co.nz

A catalogue record for this book is available from the National Library of New Zealand

Copyright © Lilla Piratförlaget AB, 2013
Original title: *Var är Pim?*
Text by Lena Landström
Illustrations by Olof Landström
Translated by Julia Marshall
Edited by Penelope Todd
Typeset by Vida & Luke Kelly, New Zealand

Printed in China by Everbest Printing Co Ltd, an accredited ISO 14001 & FSC certified printer

ISBN hardback: 978-1-927271-73-5
ISBN paperback: 978-1-927271-74-2

For more curiously good books, visit www.geckopress.com